ISBN number: ISBN 978-1-8383080-3-2

First edition May 2021
Author: Jane Huddleston
Illustrations and formatting:
David Robinson

www.sunburstcitydragons.co.uk

HARRY'S HOLIDAY

Written by
Jane Huddleston

Illustrated by
David Robinson

Outside Sunburst City, where the hills are wild and green,
Live a group of ten old dragons that most humans haven't seen.
They work and have adventures in a secret world of wonder,
While living in a hidden cave that's halfway up Mount Thunder.
They sneak around so humans don't know where they all have been,
Just two brave children help their dragon friends remain unseen.

Theo's a mechanic
Bob announces for the trains
Lucy is an athelete
Harry unblocks drains
Millie is a writer
Olive farms the land
Alice is a scientist
Jack builds chairs by hand
Yellowbeard's a pirate, now retired with creaking knees
Isla is a bee keeper, she's busy keeping bees.

HARRY

MILLIE

OLIVE

JACK

YELLOWBEARD

ISLA

Harry is a handy chap who's great at fixing drains.
He'll unblock ones stuffed full of leaves or overwhelmed with rain.
Wise and very helpful, every day he works so hard,
If he's not unblocking drains he's helping Olive in the yard.

He's 9 foot tall and chocolate brown, is strong at work and play,
But a little tired one day he thought 'I'd like a holiday!'
He walked around a rocky field that's halfway up Mount Thunder,
With gorgeous views of land and sea to think and plan and ponder.

He stopped and stood in fright as he heard voices coming near.
Frozen still against a rock he held his breath in fear.
The noise was humans laughing, Harry thought I know that sound!
His human friends were near and so he slowly looked around.

The Sunburst City dragons had two friends who were so helpful,
And in keeping dragons secret they had proven fundamental.
Matt and Alex Walker lived nearby and could be trusted,
They would often help hide dragon clues so none of them got busted.

He saw the children walking but stayed hidden and was glad,
They weren't alone, they'd come out walking with their Mum and Dad.
Standing still he listened, this weekend they had a plan.
They'd booked themselves a mini break to see the Isle of Man!

ISLE
OF
DRAGONS

DRAGON RACE SEA

LAZY DRAGON CAVES

PEEP OUT HILL

'YE WINGS OF OLD' COURT

DRAGON PASS

PORT ENID

CLAN TOWN

PORT SO SCARY

N
W   E
S

Of course, he thought, The Isle of Man! It's such a great location,
It's not too far with awesome sights, the perfect destination.
Not many people knew this Isle was not always of Man,
It was the Isle of Dragons, where there lived an ancient clan.
With hidden caves to sleep in their ancestors left behind,
He'd fly the eighty miles at night to give him peace of mind.

These dragon friends are never seen but certainly are heard,
Being expert on the telephone and at the written word.
On the far side of Mount Thunder a communication mast,
Means their internet connection's always super-duper fast.

Harry searched the internet then wrote down in a book,
Details of the super sites where he would like to look.
He packed himself a suitcase, things he could not be without,
And smiled to think his friends would love to hear his dragon shout.

At 4am he landed on the Island feeling brave.
He searched to find accommodation in an ancient cave.
He found the perfect spot, unpacked his bag and had a rest.
Then wrote a plan of where to visit and what time was best.

First he saw a water wheel still working at a mine.
Harry loved good infrastructure with robust design.
Across the Fairy Bridge he whispered 'Hello' to the Fairies,
Then headed to an ice cream shop linked to the best Manx dairies.

In the town he hid behind the Castle's ruined wall.
He saw the children so let out his secret dragon call.
They ran to him as Harry said, 'This really is a dream,
Could I trouble to you to buy me a large chocolate chip ice cream?'

Matt and Alex did so, still in shock to see their friend,
So glad their dragon buddy came to visit this weekend.
Harry said 'I read up on the mountain is the sight
Of six kindgoms, I would love it if we looked and that was right!'

The next day Harry woke up, pleased to see the sunny skies.
He flew up to the mountain and could not believe his eyes.
First the Kingdom of the Dragons, now Kingdom of Man.
Left the green of Ireland where live Aunty Enid's clan.

He looked ahead and over sea that's Scotland he was sure,
That's three I've counted now, which means I've still to count three more.
He spotted England to the right, the home he thinks is great.
Next was Wales where Griff and friends live by the Menai Strait.

He rolled his eyes remembering his gramps, it was no brag,
That his Welsh neighbours had spotted him and drawn him on their flag!
So that was five, confused the dragon spun round for a look,
Wishing he had brought with him his information book.

He took a rest, laid on the grass and gazed up to the sky,
The penny dropped 'the last Kingdom is Heaven!' he did cry.
Six kingdoms spotted, what a day and what a special place,
His friends arrived, he showed them kingdoms from his hiding space.
They talked of home, the dragon planned to fly fast over sea,
'I'm sad your trip's much slower on the ferry Ben-my-Chree'.
The children hugged their friend and went to find their dad and mum,
This holiday was perfect 'cos their dragon friend had come!

Harry told his dragon friends he loved the Isle of Man.
If he could stay well hidden he thought anybody can.
'That's it,' they said, 'next year we'll have a break from hill and heather,
To go eat ice creams in a castle, ten dragons together!'

Next time you're at a castle with a lovely big ice cream,
Just think maybe you're standing where a dragon clan have been.
Look all around, check high and low, for clues you may have missed,
For if you find a few you may prove dragons do exist!

Printed in Great Britain
by Amazon